Adam blinked and shook his head. The van was moving, rolling backwards toward the sheer drop. Jory's curly head was just visible in the driver's seat. Belinda was frozen on the hill behind, her mouth open to yell.

Adam leaped from the rock. Out of the corner of his eye he could see Marc turning from his camera toward the van. He heard his mom scream.

Adam raced across the space to the open van door. He didn't dare look behind to see how far it was from the cliff. He jumped into the driver's seat, pushing Jory out of the way, and stepped hard on the brakes. Something was wrong. They were still moving! The brakes were locked, and they were sliding on the gravel!

ASK FOR THESE TITLES FROM CHARIOT BOOKS:

ADAM STRAIGHT

TO THE
RESCUE

by K. R. Hamilton

Chariot Books
David C. Cook Publishing Co.

to Jim,
my crazy crocodillo

Chariot Books ™ is an imprint of David C. Cook Publishing Co.
David C. Cook Publishing Co., Elgin, Illinois 60120
David C. Cook Publishing Co., Weston, Ontario
Nova Distribution Ltd., Torquay, England

Cover design by Elizabeth Thompson
Cover and interior illustrations by Marcus Hamilton
First printing, 1991
Printed in the United States of America
95 94 93 92 91   5 4 3 2 1

Library of Congress Cataloging-in-Publication Data

Hamilton, K.R. (Kersten R.)
  Adam Straight to the rescue / by K.R. Hamilton.
    p. cm.
  Summary: On a camping trip in New Mexico, ten-year-old Adam
Straight finds that he likes his new stepfather and stepbrother but needs
God's help in adjusting in his stepsister.
  ISBN: 1-55513-386-X
  [1. Stepfamilies—Fiction. 2. Camping—Fiction. 3. New Mexico—
Fiction. 4. Christian life—Fiction.] I. Title.
PZ7.H1824Ad 1991
[Fic]—dc20   91-14949
                                                                  CIP
                                                                   AC

1

Adam felt the cool breeze ruffle his hair.

"Stop!" he said to his feet, but they kept moving.

He wanted to scream, but knew it wouldn't help. Then he was out of the trees, and it stretched sparkling blue before him—the pond with hundreds of paddling ducks.

"I'm dreaming," Adam said to himself. "This is just a dream."

The ducks were on the shore now, waddling toward him, yellow beaks popping, open, shut, open, shut, click, click, click!

He turned and ran back through the trees. If he could reach the house—

Adam snapped awake, damp with fear.

Ten year olds shouldn't have nightmares. Not nightmares about ducks, anyway. He started to stretch his cramped legs under the covers, then froze.

Something was moving in his room.

He jerked his blanket over his head. He had to be imagining it! What could be in his room?

Click, click, click!

Something was in his room. It was popping its teeth. Adam pinched himself to make sure he was awake.

"Mom!" He tried to speak loudly, but his voice was a hoarse whisper.

The Thing was walking now, shuffling its feet on the floor. The popping was getting closer, louder.

"I'm hungry," it growled, and before Adam could move or shout, it was on his bed, its teeth sunk into his big toe.

"Moooom!" Adam screamed as he leaped from his bed and made a dash for the door. "Mom, help!"

He slammed into the wall beside the door just as the light went on.

His mother grabbed him and hugged him.

"Adam, what's wrong? What is it, honey?"

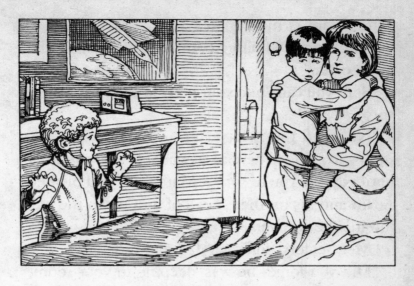

"I-I-It bit my toe," Adam stammered.

"What bit your toe?"

Adam whirled to face his bed.

A redheaded three year old in blue bunny pajamas was standing at the foot of the bed, popping his teeth.

"I'm hungry," he said.

"Jory! Did you bite Adam's toe?"

"Jory James," Marc's deep voice came from the hallway, "Did you bite Adam's toe?"

Jory showed his teeth and held his hands in front of him like claws. "I'm a meat eater," he said.

"And Adam is meat."

Marc squeezed past Adam and stood facing the meat eater.

"Son, you can't bite your new brother. Say you're sorry."

"No," said the meat eater.

"You're going to have to stay in here all by yourself until you say you're sorry," Marc said, and pushed Adam and his mother ahead of him down the hall toward the kitchen.

"Meat eaters don't care!" bellowed Jory.

"Did you forget he was sleeping in your room, honey?" Adam's mom asked.

"He jumped on my bed and bit me."

"You were having that dream again, weren't you? Do you want to pray about it?" She smoothed his hair.

Adam winced. He did want to pray about it, but not in front of Marc. No one except his mom knew about his duckmares.

"No," he said, and put his foot up on the kitchen table. The tooth marks still showed.

"I think I'll go get dressed," Marc said. "It's almost light."

When Marc had gone, Adam looked up at his mom. "I agreed to share my room with Jory for two weeks every summer, Mom. We never talked about Jory and Belinda living here all of the time."

"Life has a way of surprising us, son. I never planned on having them full time, either . . . but now that we do, we just have to work on becoming a family."

"You and me and Marc were just starting to feel like a family."

"You see! Marc and I have only been married for two months, Adam, and we already feel like a family—"

"Marc's different. He's great."

"You always wanted a brother or sister."

"I was thinking of the kind that start out little and cute with no teeth." Adam rubbed his toe. "Why did they have to come live with us all of a sudden?"

"Adam, we've been over this before. Their mom is having some problems. They've had a hard time. They have to get used to us, too. Belinda had to leave her friends and move all the way to New Mexico. Try to imagine how she feels."

"Huh."

"We need to help them feel at home. It will take more than two nights together, Adam. Give them a chance."

"Jory is okay, I guess—when he's not being a meat eater. But Belinda is weird."

"You think all ten-year-old girls are weird."

"Not like her."

"Give it time. You'll see . . . when we get back from camping, it'll seem like we've been together forever."

"We might as well get an early start," Marc said on his way past. "Want to help me with the camping gear, Adam? And Joan, don't bother messing up the kitchen cooking breakfast. We'll stop at Safari Sam's on our way out for one last civilized meal."

Adam helped load the camping gear into the back of the van.

"Well, what are we waiting for?" Marc said when they finished. "I'm ready for some breakfast!"

Someone giggled behind them. Adam turned and saw Belinda standing in the garage doorway.

"I packed my A.E.S.S., Dad."

"What's an A.E.S.S.?" Adam asked.

"My Absolutely Essential Stuff for Survival, of course," Belinda said, holding up a battered canvas bag. It looked heavy. Adam went through the kitchen, where his mom was washing Jory's face. His toe still hurt. Everyone was waiting in the van by the time he was dressed.

He walked behind them as they trooped into the restaurant.

They sure didn't look like a family.

Riley Sanches popped out the door just as Adam reached it. His family owned Safari Sam's, and Riley was almost always there.

"Hey, Adam, what are you doing up this early?" He poked Adam in the ribs.

"We're going camping in the Jemez mountains. Marc has a photo assignment from some magazine."

"Boy, it must be great having a photographer for a stepdad and a writer for a mom. They never have to go to work."

"Huh. They work all of the time."

"Sure." Riley shrugged. "You're going to be back for the party, right?"

"Party?"

Riley knocked on Adam's head.

"Hello! Is anyone home? The After School Club party. We've only been planning it every Wednesday for a month. A whole day of sun and fun at the water park, remember? And my dad said we could have ice cream on the house afterward."

"I forgot. I won't be back till Saturday night."

"How could you forget?"

"I've been kind of busy. Tell Pastor Gallegos I had to be gone, okay?"

Riley shrugged again. "You'll miss all the fun. But Marsha Motor Mouth is going, so you'll hear about everything that happens. *Everything* that happens. Gotta go. Mom's waiting in the car." Riley bounced past Adam, then turned. "Hey, Adam, what are the three fastest ways to communicate?" He didn't wait for Adam's answer. "Telephone, telegraph, and tell-a-Marsha!" He disappeared around the corner, laughing at his own joke.

Adam shook his head. Riley moved like he was made of rubber bands and chewing gum, and he told terrible jokes. But he was a good friend.

Everyone was ordering by the time Adam found their table.

When the breakfasts arrived, Belinda fished in her A.E.S.S. and brought out a big plastic jar of ketchup. She shook it twice upside down, then opened the top and squeezed a huge glob on top of her pancakes.

Adam looked around the pancake house. He was glad Riley wasn't there to watch.

Belinda smeared the ketchup around with her fork, then took a big bite of pancake dripping with red.

"That's weird," Adam said.

"So?" she said. "You have blueberry syrup. Made from fruit and sugar. Ketchup contains fruit and sugar. Tomatoes are really a fruit, you know, not a vegetable. Dad, aren't tomatoes a fruit?"

"They're a fruit, honey. Of the nightshade family, actually."

Belinda waved a fork full of ketchup and pancakes at Adam and smiled.

"You're weird," Adam said.

When they finished their breakfast, Marc took Jory to the rest room to wash his face and hands while Adam's mom paid the bill.

Adam and Belinda crawled into the back seat

of the van so Jory could sleep in the middle seat.

"I guess you've never been camping before," Belinda said as they pulled onto the freeway.

"I went once with the Scouts," Adam said.

"How long ago was that?"

"About three years, I guess." Adam didn't mention that the tent had been set up in his den mother's back yard.

"Then you don't know about them."

"About who?"

Belinda leaned toward him, her eyes wide, and whispered, "Armadiles and crocodillos."

"Armawhats and crocowhiches?"

"Shhhhh. Keep your voice down." She peeked over the back of the seat at Jory. "I'll tell you later."

Jory was showing a book of Australian animals to his stuffed Tyrannosaurus Rex. "This is a kangaroo, Wex," he growled. "It looks like you."

Adam opened the book he had brought for the trip and began to read. He managed to shut out Jory's dinosaur talk and Belinda's bouncing and was lost in his story when Belinda elbowed him.

"Jory's asleep," she said. "Now we can talk. I didn't want to scare the little guy." She glanced sideways at Adam. "Maybe I shouldn't tell you about it, either."

"Tell me what?" Adam asked.

"About *them*." Belinda lowered her voice. "Armadiles and crocodillos, that's what. They're dangerous!"

"I've never heard of them."

"Somewhere deep in the swamps of Florida, there was this pond that a big paper company kept dumping toxic waste into. You've heard of toxic waste, haven't you?"

Adam nodded.

"The animals around there started to change. Most of the things weren't too bad—birds without feathers, things like that. But somehow, an armadillo and a crocodile got mixed up. Now they are spreading like crazy, just like the killer bees in South America. You've heard of those, haven't you?"

Adam nodded again.

"Well, they're moving west. They could be in the woods where we are going. They can live in the water or on dry land, run thirty miles an hour, and jump six feet straight up in the air."

"I don't believe you."

"Dad?" Belinda called. "How high can an armadillo jump?"

"They've been known to jump six feet straight up, if they're startled."

"See?" said Belinda. "What did I tell you? Now don't mention this to my dad in front of your mom. He doesn't want to worry her. And don't tell Jory."

"I still don't believe you," Adam said.

Belinda glared at him. "I thought you would be some help," she said.

Adam turned to stare out the window. His reflection in the glass stared back at him. "God," Adam whispered, "I know I told You once that I wanted a sister, but this isn't the one."

"Who are you talking to?" demanded Belinda.

"Not you," Adam said and closed his eyes.

2

The van chugged and strained up the mountain. Adam laid his book, *John Taylor, Texas Ranger,* down in his lap. He was tired of reading. He could feel the pressure building in his ears. He yawned and felt them pop.

He had to admit that his mother had been right about the trip making them feel they had always been together. He had only been sitting on the seat beside Belinda for two hours, and it already felt like forever.

They had long since left the highway and the pavement behind, and as they climbed the steep wall of the canyon, the dust of the dry dirt road billowed behind them. Adam could see a house in the valley below. It looked like a toy. He wished the cliff was on Belinda's side of the van. She was asleep, so the sheer drop wouldn't bother her.

Captain Adam Straight of the Texas Rangers knew the short cut over the mountains was dangerous, Adam thought to himself, *but it was a chance he had to take.*

He glanced behind them. Why couldn't it have rained? The rain would have kept the dust down. But the dust was flying, curling into the sky, pointing out their location to everyone.

Had the Dalton Gang discovered his plan? Adam curled his fingers into a six gun and aimed it at a buzzard circling high above. Then he looked over his shoulder at Miz Belinda sleeping on the other side of the coach. They should never have let women like her come West. Best not fire, it might wake her up.

Suddenly the stage coach lurched to the right and came to a stop.

"Rest break," called Marc. "This is a working vacation, remember. I want some pictures of that canyon. We won't find the light just right again."

Belinda and Jory piled out of the van, and Adam followed them.

"Can I help you, Daddy?" Belinda asked.

Adam's mom was waving her notebook. "Adam,

18

I just had the greatest idea," she said. "I have to get this down before I lose it. Will you take Jory for a little walk, please?"

Jory wasn't waiting. "I'm hunting kangaroos," he called over his shoulder. Adam picked up a good walking stick and herded him away from the cliff to the bluff on the other side of the road. They found a path that was easy enough for a three year old to scramble up, worked their way around, and finally came out on top.

"Hi, Daddy," Jory called, waving.

Marc waved back. "Find any kangaroos up there?"

Adam shook his head. He set Jory up on a rock and tied his shoelaces. He didn't want the little guy to trip.

"Adam?" Jory's voice was kind of squeaky when he wasn't being a meat eater.

"Yeah, kid?"

"I like you."

Adam felt a little chokey. "Laces tight enough?"

"Yes. Adam?"

"What?"

"I'm sort of sorry."

"You're sort of sorry about what?"

"I'm sort of sorry I bit you."

"Well, it's sort of okay, so forget it."

Jory searched for kangaroos all over the hill. He looked under rocks and bushes and in a rabbit hole. No kangaroos. Then he slid back down the hill on his bottom, raining pebbles on Adam and choking him with dust.

Adam's mom was still scribbling in her notebook, and he knew better than to bother her. She never talked while she was writing.

Belinda was rooting in her A.E.S.S. Adam and Jory stopped to watch. She took out a mirror, two extra long rainbow-colored shoelaces, and three red bandannas before she found what she was looking for. Bubble gum. Adam shook his head.

"Adam, want to take a picture?" Marc called.

Adam was surprised. Apparently photographers did talk while they worked.

"Do you see the way the shadows are making the cracks on the rock face stand out, Adam? It's a beautiful picture, isn't it? Now press this button. If we wait a few moments, the light will have shifted, and it will be a totally different picture.

That's what photography is all about. Light. How we see something, how we understand it, all depends on the light we see it in."

Marc stood back from the tripod for a moment and looked around. "Where's Jory?"

Jory's head popped out from behind a bush. "I'm here, Daddy," he said.

"Come away from that edge, son." Marc turned. "Belinda! Come and watch your brother. I want you to keep him away from the edge."

"Aw, Daddy," Belinda whined. "I always have to watch Jory!"

"That's not true. Adam just took him on a kangaroo hunt."

Belinda marched Jory away, and Marc went back to his camera.

Adam pulled himself up on a boulder and laid his walking stick across his lap. He could see his mom, head bent over her notebook, tapping it with the eraser end of her pencil. She was stuck for a word.

The light had changed in the canyon, and Marc was happily clicking away.

Belinda and Jory were playing by the van.

They didn't look any more like a family than they had at breakfast.

Adam held his walking stick like a Winchester rifle.

Just his luck. A stagecoach full of gold, four tenderfeet, and the wheel has to break!

He squinted at the horizon. They could be anywhere out there. Desperados, Comancheros, the Dalton Gang. All of them wanted to get their hands on that gold. Well, they would have to get past Captain Adam Straight, Texas Ranger, first.

He stood up and spread his legs, Winchester ready.

"All right," he said to the wind. "Who wants to be first? I have bullets enough to go around!"

He heard gravel crunching behind him, and whirled. The stagecoach was rolling backwards, its door hanging open.

Adam blinked and shook his head. The van really was moving, rolling backwards toward the sheer drop. Jory's curly head was just visible in the driver's seat. Belinda was frozen on the hill behind, her mouth open to yell.

Adam threw his stick in the air and leaped from the rock. Out of the corner of his eye he could

see Marc turning from his camera toward the van. He heard his mom scream.

Adam raced across the space to the open van door. Marc was on the other side, fighting to get the passenger door open. The van was moving faster. Adam didn't dare look behind to see how far it was from the cliff. He jumped into the driver's seat, pushing Jory out of the way, and stepped hard on the brakes. Something was wrong. They were still moving! The brakes were locked, and they were sliding on the gravel!

"God, help me!" Adam didn't even realize that

he was yelling.

The van stopped with a lurch. Marc tore open the passenger door and reached over Jory to put the van in gear. "Keep your foot on the brake, Adam, while I put a rock under the tire so it can't roll."

Adam wasn't sure he could take his foot *off* the brake. His heart was pounding, and he could feel the blood racing through his body.

Finally Marc appeared at the driver's door. "It's okay now. You can let off the brake." He touched Adam's shoulder. "I said, it's okay, Adam. You can let off now."

Adam forced his foot to move. He stepped out of the van and looked back at the cliff. The rear tire was less than a foot from the edge! His knees felt weak.

Adam's mom pulled Jory from the van while Marc turned on the engine and drove back to the safe shoulder. After he had parked, he put two big rocks behind the front tires so the van couldn't roll backwards again.

"That was quick thinking, Adam," Marc said. "You saved Jory's life."

"Adam's a hero!" Jory yelled, jumping up and down.

Belinda had come down the hill.

"Belinda, where were you? I thought I asked you to watch Jory."

"I thought he would be okay in the van, Daddy. I never thought he could start it rolling."

"That part is my fault, honey. I should never have left it there without chocking the tires. But you should have been watching your brother."

"It doesn't matter whose fault it was," Adam's mom interrupted. "Thank God we're all safe." Her face was white. "That was quick thinking, Adam."

Marc didn't want any more pictures of the canyon. They loaded up the gear and headed up the mountain again.

Adam pressed his nose against the dusty window and looked at the canyon. It was a long, long way down.

"Thanks, God," Adam whispered. "I was really afraid."

Belinda was staring at him when he turned around. Tears were running down her cheeks.

"I hate you," she said. "I really hate you."

3

Are you ready, gang?" Marc asked. "This is what we're here for." He continued in his best tour guide voice. "Imagine, if you will, not the beautiful green mountain you see before you, but a giant volcano, rising thousands of feet higher than it does now.

"Imagine the pressure building up inside until it exploded, sending the entire top of the volcano into sky. The dust, dirt, and smoke affected the earth's climate for years.

"What was left behind was a crater—a huge bowl of fire—and desolation. And now, we enter the bowl of fire!"

The van pulled up over the top of the hill. A bowl-shaped valley stretched before them. Huge wasn't a big enough word for it. There were miles and miles of tall green grass, dotted with ponds, and one hill standing alone in the valley.

"The crater is called a caldera now," Marc said, "and that little hill is a resurgent dome. It came back up after the big explosion."

He backed the van into a good spot in the trees.

"Let's get busy," he said. "We want to get the tents up and firewood collected before dark."

"Meat eaters like volcanoes," growled Jory.

"Meat eaters can help gather firewood," Adam's mom said. Jory followed her into the trees, taking huge dinosaur steps.

Adam and Belinda helped Marc look for level places for the tents. They were clearing sticks and rocks from the tent sites when Belinda grabbed Adam's arm.

"Look at this," she hissed. Clearly visible in the soft dirt were some kind of animal tracks.

"They're armadile tracks," Belinda said. She squinted at them. "Or maybe crocodillo. It's hard to tell."

"I don't believe in armadiles and crocodillos," Adam said.

"Oh, yeah? We'll just see." Belinda turned her back on him.

They unfolded the tents, and Adam set the tent pegs where Marc told him to.

"You three kids will sleep in my old canvas tent." Mark rolled a big green tent out on the ground. "It's big enough for all of you, but try to be careful. The material is so old it could rip easily."

"I'm thirsty." Belinda finished whacking a peg into place. "I'm going to get a drink. Does anyone else want one?"

"No thanks, honey," Marc said. "I'll finish here first."

"How about you, Adam?" She sounded so nice, Adam blinked.

"Sure, I'd like some juice."

Adam could hear Belinda rattling around in the cooler. Had she decided to be friends?

He pounded in another stake. Well, he was willing if she was.

Suddenly icy liquid splashed on Adam's head and down his back. Crushed ice slid down his face. It was so cold he had to gasp before he could yell.

"Belinda!" he bellowed.

Marc turned to look at them. "What's going on?"

"I was bringing Adam a cup of juice, and I tripped. I'm sorry, Adam."

Adam wiped the juice from his eyes. "If you tripped, how did the juice just happen to dump right on my head?"

"Adam, go change out of your wet shirt," Marc said. "Wash off all of the juice, or it will attract gnats. Then you can go help your mother collect wood. Belinda, you stay here. You and I will finish putting up the tents."

After he'd changed, Adam walked through the

woods, kicking rocks and trees. Belinda had dumped that cup of juice on him on purpose, and she hadn't even gotten in trouble. But of course Marc would take her side. She was his kid.

He saw his mom ahead. Jory was following her, still taking dinosaur steps, his hands held in front of him like claws.

As Adam got closer, he could hear a snapping noise. The meat eater was popping his teeth! Before Adam could call a warning, the dinosaur lunged forward and sank its teeth into its prey.

"Eeeek!" Adam's mom whirled around, rubbing her bottom. "I won't stand for being bitten, young man!" She shook her finger at the dinosaur. Her face was very red.

"Meat eaters always bite their prey," Jory said.

"I'm not your prey. I'm a people, and biting hurts!"

"It will take a little while to get used to living with a meat eater, Mom," Adam commented.

"Very funny, Adam. Jory, if you're such a hungry dinosaur, you go back to camp and wait for supper. Adam, will you take him?"

Adam led the dinosaur back through the woods,

careful to stay out of the reach of his mighty jaws.

The tents were set up and waiting, so Adam hauled his sleeping bag and pack into the kids' tent. He carefully zipped the flap shut behind him. It was nice to be alone for a little while.

He unrolled his sleeping bag and put his flashlight under his pillow.

Belinda had already unrolled her bag on the other side of the tent. Her A.E.S.S. and a bowl with a huge wad of chewed gum sat beside her pillow.

Adam crawled to the door of the tent and pulled at the zipper. It was stuck. He bent over and looked at it. No fabric was caught in the runners. He tugged harder.

"What's the matter?" Belinda called from outside. "Did you get yourself stuck in there?"

"The zipper is jammed," Adam said.

"It doesn't look jammed to me."

"Well, can you give me a hand with it?"

"What's in it for me?"

"What do you mean?" Adam grunted as he pulled on the zipper.

"I mean how much money do you have with

you? If you want me to help, it will cost you two dollars."

"I don't have any money with me."

"Too bad."

Adam was getting mad. He tugged and pulled and twisted at the zipper, but not too hard. He didn't want to rip Marc's old tent. The zipper wouldn't budge.

It would be embarrassing to call for help, but he didn't have much choice.

"Mom, could you help me with this zipper?"

"Never mind, E.S., I'll help him," Belinda called quickly. She fiddled with the zipper, then unzipped it all the way to the top.

"There was nothing wrong with it," she said, as she crawled past him into the tent.

"What does E.S. stand for?" Adam asked.

"Evil Stepmother, of course."

"My mother isn't evil!"

Belinda shrugged.

"How would you like it if I called your father Evil Stepdad?"

"Who ever heard of an evil stepdad? That's a silly idea."

"I don't want you calling my mother E.S."

Belinda shrugged again and crawled out of the tent, carrying her squeeze bottle of ketchup.

On the way out, Adam stopped to examine the zipper. It worked perfectly, from the inside and from the outside. There were two tiny holes in the tent fabric beside the zipper. Adam rubbed them with his finger. How could that have affected it?

He shook his head and followed Belinda to the supper table.

After grace Adam's mom passed out tuna fish sandwiches.

Wex, Jory's stuffed dinosaur, sat beside the little boy at the table, staring at the food with black glass eyes and grinning a toothy grin.

Adam wondered how the kid could sleep with that thing. It would have given him nightmares when he was three.

Jory asked for a second sandwich. He took two bites, removed the top slice of bread, and shoved the rest of the sandwich into Wex's gaping mouth.

"Jory, you have to keep Wex clean if you're going to sleep with him," Marc said, taking the stuffed toy away from Jory and cleaning tuna fish out of its mouth. "Belinda, will you hang the trash in a tree some distance from camp? We don't want any visitors tonight."

Belinda gave Adam a knowing look and nod.

After supper, Adam stayed away from the tent as long as he could. He sat by the dying fire, trying to imagine this valley with hills of coals and glowing lakes of fire.

"Bedtime, Adam."

He couldn't put it off any longer. The tent was lit by Belinda's flashlight. Jory was already alseep in his bag, clutching Wex to his chest.

"I found more tracks," Belinda said.

"Tracks?"

"You know, armadile tracks. Or maybe they were crocodillo's. No way to be sure without killing one, of course."

"They were just wild animal tracks," Adam said.

"Armadiles and crocodillos are wild animals."

"Belinda?" Adam's mom called from the tent door. "Could I have that safety pin I loaned you? I need it after all."

"Sure, E.S.," Belinda rummaged through her A.E.S.S. and brought out a large safety pin. "I'm all done with it now."

Adam thought about the two holes by the tent zipper. If someone had pinned the outer handle of the zipper to the tent, he wouldn't have been able to open it from the inside.

Would Belinda do a mean thing like that? Dumb question.

"What did you need a safety pin for?" Adam asked.

"None of your business." Belinda turned off her flashlight.

"I don't believe in armadiles and crocodillos," Adam said. "And Belinda?"

She poked her head out of her sleeping bag. "What?"

"Stop calling my mom E.S."

4

Adam felt the cool breeze ruffle his hair.

"Stop!" he said to his feet, but they kept moving. He was back in his duckmare.

And then he saw the pond. Something had changed. A huge dark building sat on the opposite shore, smokestacks belching. Gray sludge oozed from giant pipes. And the ducks. They came paddling, just as before, yellow beaks snapping open, shut, open, shut. But they were pink and horribly featherless. Then, across the lake by the plant, Adam could see crocodiles dancing on their hind feet, swishing their tails. Armadillos appeared out of nowhere, and paw in claw with the crocodiles they waltzed toward the water.

Adam tried to turn and run, but his feet were too heavy to lift. The crocodiles and armadillos disappeared beneath the water, still dancing.

Then they were emerging on his side of the lake, but they had changed, mixed together. They all came out of the water together, pink featherless ducks, crocodillos with crocodile snouts walking on armadillo legs, armadillos with mouths full of crocodile teeth and long crocodile tails.

As Adam turned to run, he could hear the pounding, slithering, waddling horde behind him. He heard Belinda's voice saying, "Thirty miles an hour. They can run thirty miles an hour!"

Adam snapped awake.

He held his breath and listened. He could hear Belinda breathing and Jory making a little *pppt pppt* noise when he exhaled.

"I'm in a tent," he whispered to himself. "In a tent with Belinda and Jory." He felt under his pillow for his flashlight and clicked it on. The light was very dim.

He could see Belinda's sleeping bag across the tent and Jory huddled in a small ball against the back wall. Adam shook the flashlight. It grew brighter for a moment, then went off. He wished the moon were up. It would give some light.

Then he heard it. A soft scratch, scratch, scratching sound.

"I'm not going to yell this time, Jory," Adam said quietly. "Don't you dare jump on me."

Jory didn't say anything.

Adam heard a snuffling noise now, and he was sure it wasn't from inside the tent.

"Jory?" Adam whispered. "Belinda?" He could hear their soft breathing. "Belinda, wake up. There's something outside the tent, and my flashlight won't work."

Belinda grunted.

The snuffling stopped at the sound of his voice.

It started again, and so did the soft scratching sound. A scene from Adam's nightmare popped into his head—a crocodillo with powerful claws and a snout full of teeth. Adam shook his head. It couldn't be. He was not going to let his imagination run away with him.

"Belinda, I need your flashlight!"

Belinda groaned. "Go back to sleep."

"I need your flashlight. Mine's broken!"

"Too bad." This time Adam could tell she was awake.

The scratching sound had stopped; Adam hoped whatever it was had gone away. But he needed to be sure.

"Jory, are you awake?"

Jory sighed in his sleep.

Adam squirmed out of his sleeping bag and crawled to the back of the tent, shivering in the cold. He felt Jory's covers and the lump that was Jory.

Rrrriiip! Something ripped through the wall of the tent and jerked the lump out of his hand!

The thing was pulling Jory out through the back wall of the tent! Adam lunged forward and grabbed for a foot as Jory disappeared through the hole.

"Belinda, help!" Adam yelled, "It's got Jory!"

But why wasn't Jory yelling? Adam shoved his head through the tear, then squirmed the rest of the way out. He could see flashlights on in his mom's tent.

"Hurry up!" he yelled. "It's got Jory!"

Marc rushed around the corner of the tent, carrying a flashlight and a piece of firewood for a club.

Adam saw the glint of animal eyes in the light. Marc crashed into the bushes after it.

Adam's mom caught Adam from behind. "Adam, what's happening?"

Adam felt hot tears on his cheeks. "I tried to stop it, Mom, but it got away."

"What got away, Adam?"

"What's happening, E.S.?" Belinda had come around the tent with her flashlight. "Is Adam okay?"

"Why wouldn't you help me?" Adam asked, choking. "It got Jory!"

"Jory's in the tent," Belinda said calmly. "He was

in my sleeping bag with me."

Adam knees felt wobbly. "Why didn't you tell me Jory was sleeping with you when I yelled for help?"

"I was sleepy, I guess."

Jory's voice came from inside the tent. "I can't find Wex! Where did Wex go?"

"Listen," Belinda hissed. "I hear something." She tilted her head. "There's something out there."

Jory poked his head out through the rip. "What's out there, Belinda? Is it a kangaroo?"

"Both of you stop it."

Adam knew that tone of voice. His mom was getting angry.

"You're going to scare Jory."

"I'm not afraid," Jory said, crawling out of the tent. "I think a kangaroo stole Wex!"

"See what you've done? Jory, there are no kangaroos in the Jemez mountains."

Everyone could hear Marc crashing through the brush now and see glimpses of his light.

When Marc stepped out of the brush, Adam didn't know whether to laugh or to cry. Marc's shirt was half buttoned. He hadn't taken time to pull on his pants, and his bare legs glowed in the light from his flashlight. His boot laces trailed behind him. He held the firewood club in one hand and his flashlight in the other. Under his arm he carried Wex.

Adam's mom laughed. "Ugh," she said. "The mighty hunter returns!"

"Very funny." Marc didn't sound happy. "Adam, I thought I heard you say it had Jory!"

"I did! I mean, I thought it did. It would have, if he hadn't been sleeping with Belinda, and she didn't tell me when I asked her to help. . . ."

"Wex!" Jory threw himself at the stuffed dinosaur. "Wex, you're safe!"

Marc sighed. "I think it was just a misunderstanding."

"Daddy," Jory asked. "What took Wex?"

Marc picked the little boy up. "Well, son, I think it was a raccoon. I dropped my flashlight when I tripped over my boot lace, but it knew I was close behind and dropped Wex. It must have been the tuna fish Jory stuffed in Wex's mouth," Marc continued. "The raccoon must have smelled it and thought he had found himself a feast. They can be very aggressive. If you hadn't heard him stealing Wex, Adam, we would have found nothing but dinosaur scraps tomorrow morning."

"Adam saved Wex!" Jory crowed.

"The raccoon isn't likely to come back tonight, is it?" Adam's mom asked.

"Not very likely. But just to be sure, we ought to do something about Wex's tuna fish breath."

"Well, I have some mouthwash," Mom said with a laugh. "I guess it would work on a dinosaur."

Marc stitched up the tear in the tent with fishing line.

"Now let's get to sleep," he said. "It isn't even two o'clock."

Belinda was already snuggled in her sleeping bag when Adam and Jory crawled into the tent.

"Come on, Jory," she said, "keep my back warm."

"No," Jory said. "I want to sleep with Adam. Wex wants to sleep with him, too. Adam saved Wex from the kangaroo!"

"Not a kangaroo, Jory, a raccoon!"

"It was a kangaroo," Jory said. "Daddy said so."

"Daddy said raccoon," Belinda said.

"Kangaroo. Can we sleep with you, Adam? Please?"

"Oh, all right," Adam said. "Hurry up and get in the bag."

Jory scrambled into the sleeping bag and snuggled against Adam's back. It was a tight fit.

When Jory stopped wiggling and settled down, Adam was glad he was there. He felt like a little heater.

"Jory," Belinda said.

She sounded like she was crying.

"Jory, come sleep in my bag."

"No," Jory said in a sleepy voice.

"But I'm your sister!"

"Adam is my new brother," Jory said. "And he saved Wex from the kangaroos."

"There are no stupid kangaroos!" Belinda shouted.

"You kids quiet down now," Marc called.

"Yes, sir." Belinda turned off her flashlight.

Adam could hear a sniffing, hiccuping noise. Belinda was crying very softly.

Adam knew she didn't want him to hear.

5

The birds were rioting in the trees above the tent and the sun was up, but Adam didn't want to open his eyes. Jory was snuggled up to his back. Adam put his pillow over his head, and tried to go back to sleep. He was almost there, almost. . . .

A puddle of warmth spread through the sleeping bag. Then it began to cool, and Adam opened his eyes.

"Oh, no," he said.

He slid his hand down into the bag. It was sopping wet.

Jory stretched in his sleep and smiled.

"Jory, you wet the bed!"

Jory slept on.

Adam crawled out of the sleeping bag, his wet pajamas clinging to his skin.

"Did you have a little accident?" Belinda asked.

"Jory wet the bed."

"Sure, blame it on the little guy." Belinda giggled.

Adam unzipped the tent flap. His mom was working over the Coleman stove, and Marc was sitting by the fire. He couldn't get past them without being seen. Adam sighed and crawled out of the tent.

Marc looked up and smiled. "What happened to your pajamas, Adam?"

"I let Jory sleep in my bag. He wet the bed."

"You'll have to wash before you put your clothes on, honey." Adam's mom handed him a bar of soap and washcloth and pointed to the five-gallon water jug at the back of the van.

He made sure Belinda wasn't watching before he stripped off his pajamas. He washed quickly in the freezing water, dried himself, dressed, and raced to the fire before he froze.

"It's a beautiful morning, isn't it?" Adam's mom handed him a bowl of hot oatmeal.

Marc had Jory bundled in a towel. "Why did you

wet the bed, son?" he asked.

Jory looked puzzled. "I didn't," he said.

"Now, Jory," Marc cautioned.

"I didn't!" Jory opened his brown eyes wide. "Maybe it was a kangaroo!"

"Jory, it's important to tell the truth," Marc said.

Belinda crawled out of the tent carrying her ketchup bottle. "Well, maybe Jory didn't wet the bed," she said as she helped herself to a bowl of raisin oatmeal.

Adam felt his cheeks turn hot.

"Belinda." Marc's voice held a warning.

"Yes, sir." Belinda squirted a glop of ketchup into her oatmeal and stirred viciously.

The pink-gray mass with plump little raisins peeking out here and there made Adam feel queasy.

"Mom, is it okay if I take a walk?"

"Sure, honey. Stay within sight of the tent."

Adam tucked *John Taylor, Texas Ranger,* into the pocket of his jacket and started to climb the hill behind the tent.

When he could just see the camp below, he stopped and settled down on a fallen log.

The sun was warm on his back. *Captain Taylor was surrounded by desperados and running low on ammunition*. . . .

"E.S? E.S, can I borrow your hair brush?" Belinda's voice carried like a bugle in the quiet morning air. Adam slammed his book shut. Captain Taylor had never met anything like Belinda. All he had to deal with were blazing guns, bucking horses, and rattlesnakes.

"Lord," Adam said. "How could You let this happen? You know I think it's great that my mom married Marc. But God, I just can't stand that Belinda. Nobody ever said she was going to be living with us. She hates me. She hates my mom." He listened to Belinda bellowing in the camp below.

"Jesus," he said, "You've got to do something. Change something . . . please! Amen."

Adam stood up on the log and looked out over the caldera, feeling quiet inside. He let his eyes slide over the tree line. Captain Taylor always stood at the edge of a clearing, moving only his eyes, watching for movement.

He stopped. What was that? Just inside the tree line on the resurgent dome, something had moved.

Adam let his eyes slide past the spot again. Something was hunched in the shadow of the trees. It was long and low and . . . green. Adam shook his head. It couldn't be. It was too big for a raccoon or even a coyote, but too small to be a bear or deer. Belinda couldn't be telling the truth, could she? He squinted his eyes, but he couldn't make it out. It was too far away.

Adam jumped off the log and ran back to camp.

"Marc, can I borrow your binoculars? I want to get a closer look at something on the dome."

"Sure," Marc said. "They're in the van. Be careful with them."

Adam hurried back to the log with the binoculars and focused them on the dome.

The long green thing was a rock. He shook his head. "I think I'm losing my mind."

"Probably. What are you doing with my dad's binoculars?" Belinda was standing behind him with her arms folded.

"He said I could borrow them."

"Keep your voice down," Belinda said. "I need to talk to you about last night."

"I didn't wet the bed."

"Sure." She didn't sound convinced. "What really stole Wex, anyway?"

"I couldn't tell; it was too dark."

Belinda pursed her lips. "I was afraid of that. It was one of *them*, you know. Probably a crocodillo, at this altitude."

"Marc said it was a raccoon."

"He said it *might* have been a raccoon. I told you, he doesn't want to scare your mom." Belinda jumped up on the log and looked around. "Where you find one crocodillo, you'll find its mate. It would be just our luck to camp close to a lair."

"Why would they live in lairs? Armadillos don't live in lairs. Crocodiles don't live in lairs."

Belinda shrugged. "Genetic alteration, I guess. Hey, look at that." Belinda pointed. "Tracks!"

Adam set the binoculars on the log and knelt beside the prints. "They look like raccoon tracks to me," he said.

Belinda made a noise in her throat. "Right. Well, believe what you want."

"Adam!"

"Your mommy's calling you," Belinda said.

Adam turned and ran down the hill, away from Belinda.

"Yes, Mom?"

"You can help me wash out the sleeping bag at the creek." She handed him a bottle of soap.

"Mom, I didn't wet the bed."

"I know. Jory was sleeping so soundly he didn't realize he had done it."

"Yeah, but Belinda—"

"She was just teasing you, Adam. Here. You wash that side."

"She calls you E.S. Do you know what that stands for?"

"Yes. I'll just have to prove to her that I'm not an evil stepmother, won't I?"

"Huh. Mom . . . I wish you hadn't changed your last name when you married Marc."

"Are you feeling outnumbered?"

"I *am* outnumbered. One Straight and four Jameses."

"You could change your name, too."

"No. I want to keep Dad's name. And I don't want to have the same last name as Belinda!"

"So that's it. She is a handful. Adam, I remember the year your dad died, you asked for a baby for your birthday. I cried. I loved your dad so much, I was sure I would never get married again. And you would never have a brother or a sister."

"Mom." Adam didn't like it when his mother's voice sounded tight and teary. "I was two years old. I didn't know what I was saying."

"Yes . . . well." She cleared her throat. "You have a chance now to have a brother and a sister. You know, when your parents have a baby, you don't get to pick who it will grow up to be. It might be someone who is hard to live with. But when God puts a family together, He expects them to love each other, no matter what."

"Love! Mom, I can't love Belinda. I don't even like her!"

"Remember how God loved us, even when we didn't deserve it?"

"Yeah." Adam scrubbed at the bag.

"That's a special kind of love, Adam. It's called *agape*, and it's more of an action than a feeling. You don't have to *feel* like you love Belinda to have agape love for her. Not at first, anyway. Sometimes you can't choose how you feel. But you can always choose how you act." She squeezed the last bit of water from the bag lining.

"Well, that's done. Let's hang this bag over a bush. Maybe it will dry by tonight."

Adam was glad to change the subject. "I guess I shouldn't have let Jory sleep with me last night."

"Don't blame yourself. Three year olds aren't as responsible as ten year olds."

"Whoops! I left Marc's binoculars on the hill!" Adam hiked back up the hill.

Belinda was standing on the log, watching him through the wrong end of the binoculars.

"Hey, B.W.," she called, "did you forget something

when your mommy called you?"

"What does B.W. stand for?" Adam asked, although he wasn't sure he wanted to know.

"Bed Wetter," Belinda said, and smiled.

Adam clenched his fists. He wanted to punch Belinda right in her silly smile.

6

Belinda turned away from Adam and examined the caldera through the binoculars.

"This is a good place to watch for armadiles, B.W.," she said. "We can take turns."

"Don't call me B.W." Adam took a step forward. "And stop calling my mom E.S. And forget about trying to scare me with your stupid stories, Belinda. I don't believe you."

Belinda looked at him through the binoculars again. "Why don't you believe in armadiles and crocodillos?"

"I don't believe you," Adam said, "because you're a liar."

Belinda let the binoculars hang around her neck.

"I—I am not," she said.

"I think I'll ask Marc about armadiles and crocodillos this morning," Adam said.

"Don't ask him."

"Why not?"

Belinda's jaw worked, but no words came out.

Adam stared at her. What had gotten into her, anyway? Her face was pasty white.

Adam almost jumped when he heard Marc call. "There you are," Marc said as he walked up. He looked from Belinda to Adam and frowned. "Is everything all right?"

"Yes, Daddy." Belinda didn't give Adam a chance to answer.

"Well." Marc wasn't convinced. "I'm going to take a hike this morning, and I wondered if you wanted to come along, Adam."

"I'll go with you," Belinda said quickly, jumping off the log and hugging him.

"Not this time, Pumpkin."

"But, Daddy. . . ."

"I need you to stay here and help Joan take care of Jory." Marc gave her a hug. "We'll be back after lunch."

Belinda pulled away from him and ran towards camp.

"Belinda!" Marc called, but she didn't stop.

When Adam crawled into the tent to get his day pack, Belinda was sitting on her sleeping bag staring at nothing. Her face was perfectly still, but tears were running down her cheeks.

Adam turned away quickly. He found his pack and started to crawl out of the tent.

"Don't tell him," Belinda said.

Adam didn't answer.

"Look at that green," Marc said, as they hiked through the tall spring grass. "It won't be the same color this afternoon, you know. The light will be different."

"Like the light in the canyon," Adam said. "Everything depends on what light you see it in."

Marc laughed. "I'll make an artist of you yet. God knew what He was doing when He made this earth, didn't He? It's different every second."

"Yeah." Adam felt like he was walking two inches

above the grass. It was just him and Marc, like it had been before.

"Adam," Marc said, "I need to talk to you about Belinda."

Adam's feet touched down. Belinda was amazing. She could ruin things even when she wasn't there!

"Huh," Adam said.

"I know she's been making things hard for you."

Adam blinked. Marc had noticed! "She calls my mom E.S.," he said. "I wish you would make her stop."

"I know." Marc adjusted the straps on his shoulders. "We'll get around to it."

"I wish you would do it today."

"I wanted to talk to you."

"To me? Belinda's the one who needs talking to."

"Belinda's had a hard time lately." Marc stopped walking. "Adam, I need to tell you something that you can't repeat. Not even to Riley. It's the only way I know to make you understand. Will you promise me you won't talk about it, except to your mom or me?"

Adam looked Marc in the eyes. "I promise."

Marc started walking again. "You know we weren't expecting Belinda and Jory to be living with us. But their mother has been having some problems. Last week they were driving back from Denver, and she had an argument with Belinda. When they stopped for lunch in Colorado Springs, she drove off and left Belinda at the restaurant. On purpose. And she didn't come back, Adam. Belinda waited all day. She spent the night waiting outside the restaurant, in the cold. At four o'clock in the morning, when the cook came to work, he noticed Belinda and called the police, and they called me." Marc's lips were tight, and he rubbed his eyes. "You know the rest. I drove up and picked up Belinda, and then Jory. We'll get legal custody soon."

"How could she do that?" Adam asked. "Her own mother."

"I don't know. I don't know how she could do that. I called her on the phone and asked her. She said Belinda was a liar, and she couldn't live with a liar. Belinda is hurt, Adam." Marc wiped his eyes and cleared his throat. "And she's angry. She's taking all of her hurt out on you."

Adam kicked a rock.

"I wanted you to know that I know how she's treating you, and I'm proud of the way you're handling the situation."

They walked in silence around the resurgent dome.

Adam wished he could think of something to talk about, something that would take that terrible look off Marc's face. He concentrated on matching his steps to Marc's.

Finally they stopped in the shade of a juniper tree, a hundred yards from a marshy pond.

Adam helped Marc snap together his tripod,

mount the camera, and attach the cable release. Marc chose a lens from the case and screwed it onto the camera. They photographed a muskrat, then moved on.

Marc worked for an hour on a clump of tiny blue flowers.

Adam watched and helped when he could. Finally Marc stretched.

"Good grief," he said. "It's almost three o'clock! I guess I got carried away. You should have said something."

"Just like my mom." Adam laughed. "When she's writing a book, I have to fend for myself."

"Poor thing," Marc teased. "How have you survived?"

"Pizza," Adam said. "I learned to call out for pizza at a very early age."

Marc looked around. "I don't think they deliver here," he said. "You'll have to settle for peanut butter and jelly." He handed Adam a sandwich and a soda from his pack.

"We better get back and see how your mom is doing," Marc said when they had finished eating.

The walk home seemed longer in the hot afternoon, but Adam didn't mind.

He stopped and adjusted the straps on his day pack.

The valley was a different green than it had been this morning, and the sky was a deeper blue.

"You did do a good job when you made this earth, God," Adam said. "It really is different every second."

As Adam hurried to catch up with Marc, something on the resurgent dome caught the light of the afternoon sun and flashed it back.

Adam laughed.

If he hadn't been walking just where he was, if the sun hadn't been at just the right angle, if the bit of broken glass or mica on the dome hadn't been at just the right place, that flash would never have happened. It was like God was winking at him.

"Did You plan that, God?" he asked.

"What?" Marc was waiting for him.

"Nothing," Adam said as he caught up.

When they reached camp, the fire was out and the tents were zipped shut. Everything was quiet.

"Hello?" Marc called. "Joan? Belinda?"

A fly buzzed past Adam's nose.

"Where do you suppose they went?" Marc sounded puzzled.

"Daddy!" Jory bellowed as he burst from the bushes on the other side of camp.

"Marc, thank goodness you're back!" Adam's mom came right behind him. "Belinda's gone!"

7

What?" Marc pried Jory off his leg and picked him up to quiet him.

Adam's mom took a deep breath. "She said she hadn't slept well last night, and asked if she could take a nap. When I went to check on her later, she was gone."

"The kangaroo got Belinda!" Jory wailed.

"Shh, Jory, shhh. There are no kangaroos in these mountains. Belinda just took a walk. She'll be back. How long has she been gone, Joan?"

"Three hours, at least. She left this." She handed Marc a piece of paper.

He read it and then rubbed his head. "Great. Just great. Joan, can you walk along the edge of the caldera and call her? I'll look in the hills behind the tent."

"Me too, Daddy." Jory clutched Marc's neck. "I want to find Belinda!"

Marc hesitated a moment. "All right, son. You can ride in my backpack. Adam."

Adam jumped.

"I want you to stay in camp. If she comes back, don't let her leave."

"Yes, sir." Adam scratched his head. How was he supposed to stop Belinda if she wanted to leave? Tie her up?

Marc filled his canteen, set Jory in the backpack with his curly head poking out, and was gone.

"You're not worried about being here alone, are you?" Adam's mom asked.

"Of course not."

"Good. We'll find her, don't worry."

Adam watched her leave. "I'm not worried," he said, when she was too far away to hear.

The camp was quiet again. Adam crawled into the tent to get his book. Belinda's sleeping bag was rumpled and her A.E.S.S. was gone.

Adam wondered how long a person could live on bubble gum and ketchup.

"Jesus," he said, "she's just trying to get attention. She wants to ruin everything." But even as he said it, he remembered Belinda's still, white face and the tears on her cheeks.

Adam scooped up his book and crawled out of the tent. He found a good rock to sit on and started to read.

Captain Taylor was low on ammunition, but the desperados had gone. For now. He knew they were on the red bluff above him; he had seen the sun glint off the barrel of a rifle. . . .

Adam stopped reading. He couldn't get Belinda's face out of his mind. Marc had left her note on the table, and it had been blown off and caught in a bush. Adam picked it up and read it.

Daddy, it said, *you have Adam now, and you don't need a liar like me. Don't look for me. Belinda.*

"Okay, God," Adam said. "I'm sorry I called her a liar. I didn't know what had happened with her mom. I asked You to help me get along with her. I asked You to change something, remember? Belinda acts like a total brat, and I get in trouble."

So Belinda had been having a hard time. That wasn't his fault. How could her own mother call her a liar, and drive off and leave her? Families shouldn't act that way! Families should care for each other. Adam stared at the note.

There was a funny tickley feeling in his stomach. "Oh, no, God." He shook his head. "That's not fair. You want me to change, don't You? When I asked You to change something, I meant Belinda. Change *her!*"

Adam picked up a rock and threw it. "Change her!" he yelled. He picked up another rock. It felt good to throw it as hard as he could.

He threw rocks until his arm was tired, then he sat down and held his head.

Something had to change. He couldn't live with Belinda. But he didn't want to lose Marc. Somehow, they had to be a family.

"Okay, God. So You want me to be a brother to Belinda."

The sun was turning the valley golden green, changing the world again.

"God, how do You love her? She's so weird! Maybe You have a special light that makes her look more . . . more like a human."

Adam brushed a wood ant off his pants. "I know

Mom's right, Jesus. You loved me when I was still a sinner. I guess You still have to use a special light on me, so You can love me, too."

He stood up. "You win. I don't feel like a brother, but I'll try to act like a brother."

He felt worn out, but good. "I don't know why I argue with You. It's hard work." He laughed. "Besides, You always win!"

It was past dinner time and nobody was back yet, so Adam gathered enough dry wood for the evening fire, then picked up his book and tried to read. *The sunlight flashed off the barrel of. . . . The sunlight flashed. . . .*

Adam jumped up. "I know where she is," he said. It was just like Belinda. She had been watching them the whole time, through the binoculars, from the top of the resurgent dome.

"Okay. If I were a real brother, what would I do?"

It was almost sundown. She shouldn't stay out all night, alone. It only took Adam a moment to decide. A real brother would go find Belinda.

He left a note stuck under the windshield wiper of the van, explaining where he had gone, then started trotting across the valley.

When he reached the dome and started to climb, he moved more carefully.

"Captain Adam Straight, Texas Ranger, always gets his man . . . or girl," Adam said. His voice sounded strange in the quiet. "Nothing can stop him. Desperados . . . wilderness . . . animals." Adam heard a rustling in the bushes behind him. He whirled.

"Belinda?" he called. "Is that you?"

Nothing.

He picked up a sturdy branch. "Captain Straight is afraid of nothing," he said. He stepped forward, club ready.

Just as he reached the bush, a rabbit exploded out of it and raced across his feet. "Yikes!" Adam jumped back, almost dropping his club.

"Great," he said. "Captain Adam Straight, scared of a rabbit." He dropped the branch and started up the hill again.

At the very top he found a clearing. Someone had gathered a pile of dry wood for a fire and bent the branches of a small fir tree together to make a shelter. The branches were tied with a pair

of rainbow shoelaces.

Looking back toward camp, Adam could plainly see the tents and the van. He could even tell that no one was back yet.

What a perfect place to spy from. Belinda must have watched his mom looking for her all afternoon. She could have watched him throwing rocks and pacing the camp. And she would have seen him coming.

A normal person would have avoided him and gone back to camp. Adam shook his head. Belinda was definitely not normal. She might have decided to run away for good and headed down the other side of the hill.

Adam glanced west. The sun had dropped out of sight, but there would be light for more than half an hour. If he ran, he could check the back of the dome, just to be sure, and be back at camp before dark. Maybe.

Adam started jogging, moving through the brush as quickly as he could. He was halfway down the hill when he saw a flash of yellow through the trees.

Belinda's jacket! Adam stopped jogging and tried to breathe evenly. If she heard him coming, she might run again.

But Belinda wasn't running down hill, she was limping back up, her A.E.S.S. dragging in the dirt behind her. Her face was pale and tear-streaked.

"Belinda," Adam said as she got closer. "I'm sorry I called you a liar."

"Shut up, B.W."

Adam frowned. Something was wrong with Belinda's foot. One tennis shoe was white, but the other was red and wet looking.

Belinda took another step toward him, and blood oozed over the top of her shoe.

8

Belinda, what happened?"

"I cut my foot, B.W., what does it look like?"

"It looks bad. Sit down."

"Why should I?"

"Because we have to stop the bleeding." Adam pulled her walking stick away from her. She hopped on one foot for a moment and then sat down.

Adam loosed the laces, pulled her shoe off, and poured the blood out of it. It smelled sweet and raw, and Adam felt like gagging. He swallowed hard, then stripped off her sock so he could see the cut. Blood was slowly pumping from it.

"Give me a bandanna."

"What for?" Belinda sounded sullen, but she pulled a bandanna out of her A.E.S.S.

72

"I'm going to have to press on the cut." Adam folded the bandanna into a square and pressed it directly on the cut.

"Ouch! Stop that!" Belinda wiggled.

"I have to press on it until the bleeding slows down," Adam said. He didn't let go of her foot. "How did you cut it?"

"Running away from you. Some idiot broke a beer bottle on the rocks, and the glass punched right through my shoe. Did you take a class in first aid?"

"No. But when John Taylor's buddy Lando got shot in the foot by Billy the Kid—"

"You mean you got this out of one of your stupid books? Great, B.W., you're probably going to kill me—ouch! Can you stop pressing on it yet?" She sat up to look at her foot.

"Not yet. It doesn't stab when I press on it, does it? My mom says that if there is glass left in a cut, it feels like it's stabbing you when you press on it."

"No, it just stings. B.W., don't hold it up so high!"

"I have to elevate it; it will help stop the bleeding. Lie down. And stop calling me B.W."

Belinda lay down and closed her eyes.

Adam held the bandanna in place until his fingers were tired, then he looked at the cut again. The blood wasn't pumping anymore, but it was still bleeding a little. He put the bandanna back and pressed some more.

It was getting dark.

"Do you have a flashlight?" Adam asked.

"No. I forgot it under my pillow."

Adam thought hard. "As soon as I can let go of your foot, I'm going to leave you here and go get your dad. You can't walk back to camp." He hoped he could find his way in the dark.

"B.W.!" Belinda straightened up. "You have to stay here!"

"I'll bring Marc right back."

"Stay here!" Belinda's voice sounded strange. "I don't want you to go!"

"You'll be okay."

"B.W., please. I'm . . . I'm afraid of the dark." Belinda didn't look at him. She stared up at the first star that had appeared in the sky. "I don't want to be out here all alone."

"But you ran away. You were going to spend the night out here alone."

"Don't go."

Adam sighed. "All right. I left a note. As soon as they read it, they'll know where we are and come find us."

The light disappeared quickly, and the darkness around them was like no darkness Adam had ever been in before. If he hadn't been holding Belinda's foot, he wouldn't have known she was beside him.

He stared at the stars and wished the moon were up.

A coyote yipped somewhere, and Adam jumped. If he could smell the blood from Belinda's foot, then every animal for miles around could probably smell it.

With one hand he felt around on the ground for Belinda's walking stick.

"What are you doing, B.W.?"

"Nothing," Adam said.

Then he heard a whistle.

"That's my dad!" Belinda's foot wiggled excitedly, and she whistled back, long and loud.

A few more minutes, and they could see the glow of Marc's flashlight.

"We're over here!" Adam yelled.

"What happened?" Marc asked, as the beam from his flashlight hit Belinda. "Belinda, are you okay?"

"No." Belinda heaved herself up to her elbows. "Adam chased me right into a broken beer bottle, and I cut my foot."

Marc took the foot from Adam and examined it while Adam held the light. "Looks like you're going to need stitches," he said. "Adam, you did just right, stopping the bleeding."

Adam felt his face grow hot. He was glad it was dark. But wasn't Marc going to say anything to Belinda about running away?

"I'm going to make a tight bandage out of your bandannas, and then I'll give you a piggy back ride back to camp, honey," Marc said.

When they reached the camp, Adam's mom was pacing in the light of a Coleman lantern.

"Adam, you were told to stay in camp! What do you mean by running off like that!"

"Belinda's cut her foot, Joan," Marc interrupted. "Adam managed to stop the bleeding, but I'm going to have to drive her over the mountain to the emergency room at Los Alamos. I think she's going to need stitches."

"We could pack up camp—"

"No, that would take too long. I want to have this foot looked at. You three might as well get a good night's sleep. We'll be back in a few hours if it isn't too serious. At worst, I'll come pick you up tomorrow morning. Will you be okay here?"

"Don't worry, tough guy," Adam's mom said. "I can fight off the raccoons tonight."

"I want to go with you, Daddy!" Jory said.

"I need you to take care of Joan and Adam for me, Jory. Can you do that?"

Jory looked at Adam, then nodded.

Marc put Belinda in the front seat of the van, kissed Jory, and left.

Adam scrubbed the blood off his hands.

"Adam, we still need to talk about your leaving camp," Adam's mom started before the van was out of sight.

"I knew where Belinda was, Mom."

"But Marc told you not to leave. You should have waited for one of us to come back. If you hadn't been chasing her she wouldn't have cut her foot."

Adam wished he were at home. He felt like slamming a door. "How come I get in all the trouble, when Belinda is the one who ran away? I was trying to act like a real brother. Well, Belinda doesn't want another brother. Not me, anyway."

Jory's lower lip was sticking out. "I want my daddy," he said.

"Oh, Adam." Mom gave him a quick hug. "I'm proud of you for trying. But I was so worried about you. Come on, let's roast some marshmallows. Do you want a marshmallow, Jory?"

Jory dragged Wex over to the fire and watched

78

with big eyes while Adam roasted marshmallows.

Soon the little boy's head was bobbing.

"Looks like Jory's ready for bed, and so am I." Adam's mom picked Jory up. "He's just like you when you were three, Adam."

Adam didn't believe that. He'd never had a stuffed Tyrannosaurus Rex, and he'd never worried about kangaroos.

Adam helped tuck Jory in and watched him sleep for a moment before he turned out Belinda's flashlight. "Poor little guy," he whispered. "I'd probably have worried about kangaroos, too, if I'd had a sister like Belinda."

Adam knew he had been duckmaring, but somehow he couldn't remember the dream. Someone was crying, very softly. The moon was so bright that he could see even inside the tent. The sobs were coming from Belinda's sleeping bag. So they had come back after all. Belinda had the bag pulled up all the way over her head, and it shook every time she sobbed. In the dim light it looked like a very sad caterpillar.

"When did you get back?" Adam whispered.

The caterpillar stopped shaking.

"So, what did my dad say when you asked him about armadiles and crocodillos?"

"I forgot to ask. How's your foot?"

"Five stitches, thanks to you," she said. "Why don't you take a long hike? There's still time for a bear to eat you before morning."

"I'm not going for a walk," Adam said. "I'm sorry you got cut, but it wasn't my fault you stepped on that broken bottle. You can poke your head out. The moon is up, so it isn't really dark in here."

"I don't care," Belinda said. The caterpillar wiggled.

"Everybody is afraid of something," Adam said.

"Shut up, B.W. What would you know about anything? Mr. Perfect Hero, saving Jory's life, saving Wex. I hate you."

"I do know about being afraid. I'm afraid of ducks." It was out of Adam's mouth before he thought.

The caterpillar hiccuped. "What?" it said.

"Nothing."

"You said you were afraid of ducks, didn't you, B.W.?" The sleeping bag wiggled towards him, and he thought he could see the glint of eyes peering from within. "Why would anyone be afraid of ducks?"

"When I was just a baby, we were feeding bread crumbs to some ducks. One duck grabbed my hand," Adam said defensively. "I have a scar, see?" He held his hand toward her. "I don't really remember it, but I still have nightmares."

Belinda's head popped out of her sleeping bag. She stared at Adam for almost a minute.

"Go to sleep, B.W.," she said. She pulled her head back into the sleeping bag and inched to her side of the tent.

"Jesus," Adam prayed, "Why did I say that? I'm doomed."

"What?" Belinda demanded.

"Nothing," Adam said.

"You sure do talk to yourself a lot," Belinda said. "You are definitely weird."

9

By the time they'd taken down the tents, packed the van, and cleaned up the campsite, it was past noon.

Adam squirmed. They were leaving the bowl of fire behind, but he felt like he was taking it home with him, right in his middle. If Belinda could cause this much trouble on a camping trip, what was it going to be like living with her?

He squirmed again, trying to make more room. The short middle seat was not big enough for two boys and a Tyrannosaurus.

"How's the foot, honey?" Marc called over his shoulder.

"It's okay."

Belinda was stretched across the whole back

seat, her cut foot on a pillow, cracking sunflower seeds with her teeth and spitting the shells into a cup.

"Good. We need to take the long way home, over the mountain, so I can get some pictures of the lava beds at Grants."

Jory pressed his nose to the window. "Goodbye, kangaroos," he said in his dinosaur voice.

When they stopped at the lava beds, Adam's mom upacked the cooler. "We might as well use up this food," she said. "We can eat dinner right here."

Adam ate the sandwich she handed him and thought about the party he was missing. Riley, Beth, and Marsha were probably having a great time. He wished he were with them, splashing in the cool water, instead of sitting on a hot black rock with Belinda.

When Marc was finished taking pictures, he called, "All aboard! Next stop Albuquerque. We'll be home in an hour!"

The van was quiet all the way back. Jory was sleeping, and Belinda was writing in a notebook she had pulled out of her A.E.S.S. Adam finished *John Taylor, Texas Ranger.*

"Hmmm," Marc said as they pulled off the freeway. "I feel like ice cream. How about you?"

"Is this another tradition?" Adam's mom asked. "Pancakes when we leave and ice cream when we get back?"

"Why not?" Marc pulled into Safari Sam's parking lot.

"What a trip," Adam's mom said. "I hope we don't make such exciting camping trips a tradition. I don't think I could take it."

"Let's hope not," Marc laughed.

Adam walked behind them into the restaurant.

They looked just like they had two days ago at breakfast, except now Belinda was limping.

"Adam, isn't that your After School Club over there?"

Adam nodded. "We were going to meet here after the swim party. Riley's dad was giving us free desserts."

"Why don't you take Belinda over and introduce her to the kids?"

"I don't know."

"Oh, go on." She gave him a little shove. "You can order dessert with them. Look, there's Riley!"

Adam crossed the room, Belinda hobbling behind him. Riley made room for him, and Adam scooted into the booth.

"Hi, guys," he said. "I'd like you to meet—"

"Belinda," Belinda said. "Move over and let me in."

Please, God, Adam prayed, *don't let her—*

"I said move over, B.W.," Belinda said. "I need room for my foot."

Adam groaned.

"Hey," said Marsha, "those aren't your initials. What's it stand for?"

"Are you ready to order?" Riley's older sister was working as a waitress. She blew a bubble with her gum and popped it as she took their orders.

"You should have gone with us, Adam," Riley said. "It was great!"

"Yeah?" Adam edged a little further from Belinda.

"I went down the Human Bullet slide," Riley began.

"And we all had pizza for lunch. Tammy was there—you know, from school—and. . . ." Marsha was off. She was describing the toppings Tammy had ordered on her pizza when Riley's sister arrived with the ice creams and sodas.

Riley tore the end off his straw wrapper and shot it across the table. It hit Marsha in the ear, but she didn't even pause for breath. "And Pastor Gallegos wouldn't let Riley in the water after he ate six pieces of pizza. . . ."

Riley chewed part of his napkin into a spit wad and aimed it at Marsha's nose. But he stopped in mid-shot.

"What's she doing?" he asked, pointing his straw at Belinda.

Belinda was squirting ketchup on her ice cream. She stirred it around and took a big bite before she noticed that everyone was watching her.

"Is she really a friend of yours, Adam?" Marsha asked in a loud whisper. She had forgotten the swim party.

"Yeah," Beth added. "Who is she?"

Belinda sat straighter and ignored them. The color was draining from her face.

Adam frowned. She didn't deserve any help. But his tummy was tickling again. He tried to ignore

it, but it got worse.

Okay, Jesus, okay, he prayed silently. *What should I do? What would a real brother do?* His mind was blank. The silence lasted a little too long. He had to do something.

"She's . . ." Adam took a deep breath. At any moment, Belinda would call him B.W. again, and Marsha would ask what it meant, and as soon as she knew, Adam's life would be over. He couldn't go back to school next fall if everyone was calling him Bed Wetter. He couldn't play soccer or meet with the After School Club. He would never leave his room again.

But he had said he would try. Everyone was staring at Adam now.

"She's my stepsister," he said. His voice sounded kind of squeaky. He cleared his throat. "Say, Belinda, will you pass the ketchup?"

Belinda slid the ketchup bottle down the counter, and Adam held it over his vanilla ice cream. He tried not to shudder as he squeezed a glop out.

"Tomatoes are really a fruit," he said as he stirred. "You know, like . . . strawberries."

He hoped it wouldn't taste as bad as it looked.

It did.

He rolled it around on his tongue. "Hmmm, interesting," he said.

Riley blinked.

"Dis-gus-ting," he said happily, and reached for the ketchup. He squirted a glop into his shake.

Beth turned to Belinda. "I didn't know Marc had a kid our age. Are you going to be living at Adam's house?"

Good old Beth. She would be nice to a bloodthirsty monster.

"Yeah, I'll be living with B.W."

Adam winced.

"So, after you finished lunch?" he said. "C'mon, Marsha, what happened next? Did h. really do the Human Bullet?"

Marsha smiled. "Well . . ."

Adam let his ice cream melt in the bowl as Marsha finished her story.

"Adam! Belinda! We have to go," Marc called.

"See you guys later." Adam pushed Belinda out of the booth. "We have to get home."

Riley waved his straw at them and smiled.

"Hey, Belinda," Marsha called after them. "What were you calling Adam? P.W.? You know, when you first came in?" But Belinda was already out the door.

Adam bit his lip. His life was over. It was only a matter of time.

10

Adam, Belinda wants to go for a bike ride," Adam's mom said. "Why don't you go with her? She can ride your old bike, and you can show her around."

Adam knew his mother's this-would-be-a-good-idea voice when he heard it.

"Sure, Mom." He moved like a robot, wheeling the bikes out of the garage. It was a beautiful morning, but Adam didn't care.

Marsha could appear at any moment, and it would all be over.

Belinda would ruin his life.

"Ready, B.W.?" Belinda grinned. "You don't have to show me around. I know just where I want to go."

Before they had gone six blocks, Adam knew

where she was heading. He wanted to turn back, to pump his pedals hard all the way home. But if he did that, Belinda would tell Marsha. And Marsha would tell the world.

Adam would have screamed, but he knew it wouldn't help.

They parked their bikes by a tree.

His feet seemed to move by themselves. *Stop, feet!* Adam thought desperately. *STOP!* But they kept on moving.

The pond stretched sparkling blue before him.

The ducks were in the water. They paddled toward him, beaks open, quacking hungrily.

His feet finally got the message and stopped, but the ducks were already out of the water, waddling up onto the shore.

Adam turned and ran . . . right into Belinda.

"Well, B.W.," she said, "what's it going to be?"

The ducks waited, beady eyes blinking.

Adam rubbed his sweaty palms on his jeans. "Shoo," he said.

The ducks shuffled from foot to foot, uncertain.

"Shoo!" Adam said a little louder, waving his arms.

The ducks backed up.

Adam took a step forward. "Get outta here," he yelled, and this time the ducks turned and started for the water.

Adam took another step. He could see Belinda out of the corner of his eye, always one step behind him.

The ducks were running from him. They were afraid of him! Adam whooped and chased them all the way to the water's edge.

It felt good, really good.

"Hey, you guys!"

The good feeling disappeared. Marsha and Beth were walking toward them.

"Hey, you guys," Marsha said again. "What are you doing?

"B.W.'s showing me around," Belinda said.

"Adam, are you feeling okay?" Beth asked. "You look kind of sick."

Adam couldn't speak.

"Oh, B.W.'s all right," Belinda said. "He just got out of bed too early."

"B.W.," Marsha squealed. "*That's* what you were calling him at Safari Sam's last night. I've been trying to remember all morning, so I could ask you. What's it stand for, anyway?"

Adam's face burned. This was it. The end had come.

"Adam, why is your face so red? Are you sure you feel okay?" Beth took a step toward him.

"Oh, he's okay. He doesn't want you to know what B.W. stands for, that's all."

Marsha leaned toward Belinda. "What does it stand for?"

"I'll tell you for five dollars," Belinda said.

"I don't have five dollars."

"Come on, Marsha." Beth pulled on Marsha's arm. "If Adam doesn't want us to know—"

"I have a dollar and twenty cents," Marsha said.

"Okay," Belinda said, "Hand it over, and I'll tell."

Adam watched as Marsha counted the money into Belinda's hand. A dollar and twenty cents. His life was worth more than a dollar and twenty cents!

"I'll give you five dollars not to tell," he said.

Belinda smiled as she shoved Marsha's money into her pocket.

"Don't be shy, B.W. They really should know."

She flung her arm around Adam's shoulders, but he didn't feel it. He was numb.

"B.W. stands for—" she paused dramatically. "Boy Wonder!"

"What?" Adam jumped.

"Boy Wonder," Belinda said again.

"Boy Wonder? Why would you call him Boy Wonder?" Marsha demanded.

"Because he saved my little brother from a crocodillo."

"I didn't save Jory, it was Wex—" Adam started.

"He fought it off singlehanded," Belinda said.

"What's a crocodillo?" Marsha asked.

94

"It's a mix between an armadillo and a crocodile. They're very dangerous."

"Really?" Marsha stared at her. "And Adam fought one off?"

Belinda smiled. "Saved Jory's life."

"That's really great, Adam," Beth said. "You saved a little kid!"

"It was a raccoon," Adam said, but no one was listening.

Marsha was dragging Beth away. "Come on, Beth, we have to tell everybody. Adam's a hero! Bye, Belinda! Bye, Boy Wonder!"

Adam took a deep breath. It was better than Bed Wetter.

Marsha was still staring over her shoulder at the Boy Wonder as she and Beth turned the corner.

Belinda smiled and waved.

"Why did you tell them it was a crocodillo?" Adam asked. "You don't really believe in armadiles and crocodillos, do you?"

Belinda frowned. "Of course not. What do you think I am, crazy?"

"No, but why . . . oh, never mind. Thanks for not telling them . . . you know."

"Don't get mushy." Belinda folded her arms. "I owed you two. The ducks—that was for staying with me when I cut my foot. Even if it was your fault. And I owed you one for last night, when you didn't let your friends laugh at me. So . . . I'll admit that it *might* have been Jory who wet the bed."

Adam felt like laughing. Maybe he could live with Belinda after all.

"It might not be so bad, having a sister," he said.

"Who said I was your sister?!" Belinda bellowed. She whirled and hobbled down the shore after the ducks, shouting and spinning her arms like a windmill.

Adam watched the ducks scattering before her.

"Well, Jesus," he said. "Well . . . I guess it's a start."